# Blast Off!

## The Sound of BL

By Alice K. Flanagan

The Child's World®

When a rocket takes off, say "blast off!"

A rocket looks like
a blur in the sky.

When an airplane
lifts off, say "blast off!"

An airplane leaves
the trees and
the bluffs behind.

When a racecar zooms away, say "blast off!"

If you blink, you might miss the car as it zooms by.

When fireworks
are shot into the sky,
say "blast off!"

Do not let the black
and blue smoke get
in your eyes.

When a space shuttle
leaves Earth,
say "blast off!"

Say "blast off" and
wave goodbye!

# Word List

black

blast

blink

blue

bluffs

blur

# Note to Parents and Educators

Welcome to Wonder Books® Phonics Readers! These books are based on current research that supports the idea that our brains detect patterns rather than apply rules. This means that children learn to read more easily when they are taught the familiar spelling patterns found in English. As children progress in their reading, they can use these spelling patterns to figure out more complex words.

The Phonics Readers texts provide the opportunity to practice and apply knowledge of the sounds in natural language. The ten books on the long and short vowels introduce the sounds using familiar onsets and *rimes*, or spelling patterns, for reinforcement. The letter(s) before the vowel in a word are considered the onset. Changing the onset allows the consonant books in the series to maintain the practice and reinforcement of the rimes. The repeated use of a word or phrase reinforces the target sound.

As an example, the word "cat" might be used to present the short "a" sound, with the letter "c" being the onset and "–at" being the rime. This approach provides practice and reinforcement for the short "a" sound, since there are many familiar words with the "–at" rime.

The number on the spine of each book facilitates arranging the books in the order in which the sounds are learned. The books can also be arranged into groups of long vowels, short vowels, consonants, and blends. All the books in each grouping have their numbers printed in the same color on the spine. The books can be grouped and regrouped easily and quickly, depending on the teacher's needs.

The stories and accompanying photographs in this series are based on time-honored concepts in children's literature: Well-written, engaging texts and colorful, high-quality photographs combine to produce books that children want to read again and again.

Dr. Peg Ballard
Minnesota State University, Mankato, MN

# About the Author

Alice K. Flanagan taught elementary school for ten years. Now she writes for children and teachers. She has been writing for more than twenty years. Some of her books include biographies, phonics books, holiday books, and information books about careers, animals, and weather. Alice K. Flanagan lives with her husband in Chicago, Illinois.

**Published by The Child's World®**
PO Box 326
Chanhassen, MN 55317-0326
800-599-READ
www.childsworld.com

**Photo Credits**
© Alan Schein Photography/Corbis: 13
© Bill Aron/Photo Edit: 18
© Corbis: cover
© David Lawrence/Corbis: 6
© Dennis MacDonald/Photo Edit: 14
© F.J.Hooker/Corbis: 5
© Reuters NewsMedia,Inc./Corbis: 10
© Richard Hutchings/Photo Edit: 17
© Roger Ressmeyer/Corbis: 2
© Rolf Bruderer/Corbis: 21
© Tony Freeman/Photo Edit: 9

The Child's World®: Mary Berendes, Publishing Director
Editorial Directions, Inc.: E. Russell Primm, Editorial Director and Line Editor;
Alice K. Flanagan/Flanagan Publishing Services, Photo Researcher, Linda S. Koutris, Photo Selector

**Library of Congress Cataloging-in-Publication Data**
Flanagan, Alice K.
  Blast off! : the sound of BL / by Alice K. Flanagan.
    p. cm. — (Wonder books)
Summary: Simple text features words that contain the consonant blend, "bl."
  ISBN 1-59296-154-1 (Library Bound : alk. paper)
  [1. English language—Phonetics. 2. Reading.] I. Title. II. Series:
Wonder books (Chanhassen, Minn.)
PZ7.F59824Bl 2004
  [E]—dc22
                        2003018099

24